W9-AYG-676

ADVENTURES OF

THE BLACK HOLE GANG

THE DARK ZONE

EXPLORING THE SECRET WORLD OF CAVES

BY STEPHEN KRAMER
ILLUSTRATED BY RICHARD TORREY

LEARNING TRIANGLE PRESS
An imprint of McGraw-Hill

New York San Francisco Washington, D.C. Auckland Bogotá
Caracas Lisbon London Madrid Mexico City Milan Montreal
New Delhi San Juan Singapore Sydney Tokyo Toronto

McGraw-Hill

A Division of The McGraw·Hill Companies

pbk 1 2 3 4 5 6 7 8 9 MAL / MAL 9 0 3 2 1 0 9 8
ISBN 0-07-036920-8

Library of Congress Cataloging-in-Publication Data
Kramer, Stephen.
    The dark zone: adventures of The Black Hole Gang / Stephen Kramer.
        p. cm.
    Summary: Four kids interested in science learn through the Internet of a vandalized cave that needs cleaning up and have an unusual adventure.
    ISBN 0-07-036920-8
    1. Science—Comic books, strips, etc.—Juvenile literature.
[1. Science—Fiction. 2. Caves—Fiction. 3. Cartoons and comics.]
I. Title.
PN6727.K68D37   1998
741.5'943—DC21

97–32644
CIP
AC

McGraw-Hill books are available at special quantity discounts. For more information, please write to the Director of Special Sales, McGraw-Hill, 11 West 19th Street, New York, NY 10011. Or contact your local bookstore.

Acquisitions editor: Judith Terrill-Breuer
Production supervisor: Clare B. Stanley
Designer: Jaclyn J. Boone

BHG

BAT RESOURCES

Kramer, Stephen. *Caves*. Minneapolis, MN: Carolrhoda Books, 1995.

Schultz, Ron. *Looking Inside Caves and Caverns*. Santa Fe, New Mexico: John Muir Publications, 1993.

Bat Conservation International: www.batcon.org

DEDICATIONS

For Edythea Ginis Selman:
agent, muse, and friend.
— S.K.

For Sue, Heather, and Drew.
And for Doc.
— R.T.

ACKNOWLEDGMENTS

Many people have contributed to this book. Charlie Larson, of Western Speleological Survey, has always been willing to answer my questions about caves and provided me with information on cave clean-up techniques. Jim Nieland, USFS Cave Management Specialist, and his wife Libby made helpful suggestions about story ideas and explained cave gates to me. Bill Torode, National Speleological Society Librarian, tracked down information on Luella Agnes Owen and Ruth Hoppin. Norma Elizondo, Lilian and Iris Yung, Fred and Eunice Kramer; and Tim and Ruth Kramer contributed ideas and suggestions for naming *The Black Hole Gang* members.

Finally, much of what I've learned about caves and cave conservation is a result of my association with the National Speleological Society. I'd like to encourage anyone with a further interest in caves, caving, and cave conservation to contact the NSS for more information:

National Speleological Society
2813 Cave Avenue
Huntsville, Alabama 35810—4431

www.caves.org

— S.K.

In some ways, the Millers seem like such a normal family.

In other ways, however, they have a reputation for being a bit odd.

1

Mr. Miller works at the university. That doesn't seem so unusual.

Mrs. Miller works at the university too. And that doesn't seem so unusual.

But the Millers are a little different.

Matt has always been crazy about science.

He built his own telescope when he was nine years old, and he's been using it ever since.

Matt's friends A.J., Wei Ling, and Rosa also loved science. They decided to build a clubhouse in the Miller's backyard, so A.J. drew up some plans.

Matt, Wei Ling, Rosa, and A.J. used the clubhouse to do experiments, read about science, and work on their collections. Sometimes they put on programs for the neighborhood kids.

They began calling themselves The Black Hole Gang. Even when they weren't doing science, they were usually talking about it.

The neighborhood kids soon learned where they could find answers to their science questions.

Matt, A.J., Rosa, and Wei Ling even got questions and notes from other parts of the country.

Dear Black Hole Gang,

My teacher gave us a science homework assignment. We're supposed to find out what a megabat is. I've checked in my science books, but I can't find the answer. Can you help?

Dear Carl,

Most bats are small, but some species—called megachiropterans, or megabats—can grow to be five feet from wing tip to wing tip. Because of their fox-like faces and large size, some are called flying foxes. Most of these bats eat fruit. Ask your teacher to take you on a field trip to see some wild megabats. Your class would have to go to tropical Asia, Africa, Australia, or the South Sea Islands to find them!
    Sincerely,
    Wei Ling

Dear Black Hole Gang,

I have a terrarium in my bedroom. It has grass, flowers, and a mushroom from our backyard growing in it. My family went on vacation during spring break. When we got back, I found a blanket on my terrarium. Before we left, my little brother had covered it "so the plants wouldn't get cold." The green plants were practically dead. They looked terrible, but the mushroom was fine.
What happened?

Dear Natalie,

All living things need energy to grow and stay alive. Little brothers (and other animals) get energy from food. Green plants use a chemical called chlorophyll to capture energy from sunlight. Mushrooms get their energy by breaking down chemicals in the soil or the wood they grow on. That's why your mushroom survived under the blanket and your green plants had trouble. If you get your terrarium back into the sunlight, your green plants will probably recover.
A.J.

A.J. sold some of his extra plants.

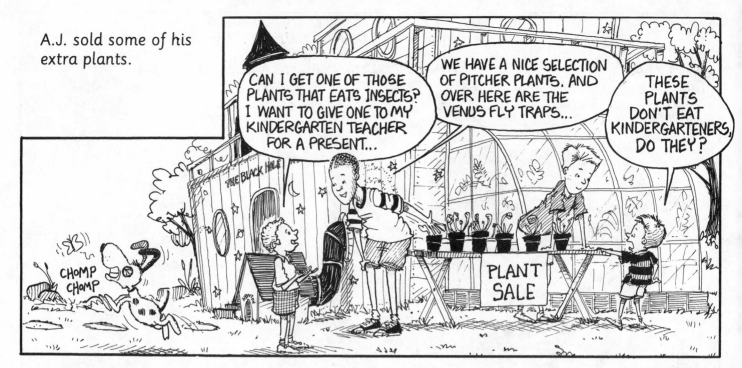

Wei Ling sold some of her watercolor paintings.

And everyone helped with the dog wash . . .

Rosa, Matt, and Mr. Miller gave the truck a tune-up.

By the time Matt explained the plans to his mother—
and told her about all the work everyone had done to get ready—
it would have been hard for her to say no.

So, the day after school let out for the summer,
The Black Hole Gang headed for Missouri.

Five days, 2379 miles, and 60 ice cream cones later,
The Black Hole Gang arrived at the farm.

It didn't take long for Lindsey to become friends with Wei Ling, Rosa, A.J., and Matt.

Later in the day . . .

After the dinner dishes were washed, Matt and A.J. did a little tree climbing . . .

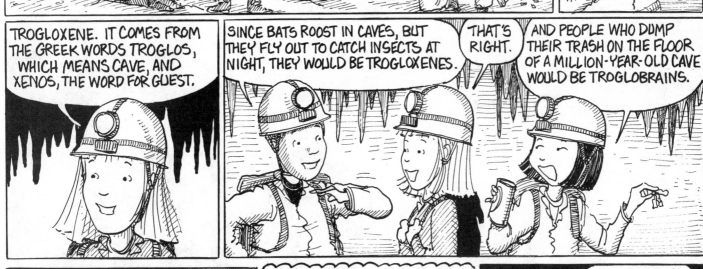

THAT'S RIGHT. BUT SOIL CONTAINS DECAYING PLANT PARTS-- ROOTS, STEMS, BRANCHES, AND LEAVES...

...WHEN THESE PLANT PARTS DECOMPOSE, THEY GIVE OFF CARBON DIOXIDE GAS-- WHICH COLLECTS IN UNDERGROUND SPACES IN THE SOIL.

CARBON DIOXIDE GAS

CARBON DIOXIDE-- THAT'S CO_2.

WHEN WATER TRICKLES THROUGH THESE POCKETS OF CARBON DIOXIDE, IT CHANGES...

SCRUB SCRUB

...THE WATER BECOMES A WEAK ACID CALLED CARBONIC ACID.

WATER

CARBON DIOXIDE

CARBONIC ACID

THAT'S H_2CO_3. TWO ATOMS OF HYDROGEN, ONE ATOM OF CARBON, THREE ATOMS OF OXYGEN.

SCRUB SCRUB

HOW CAN SHE REMEMBER ALL THOSE CHEMICAL FORMULAS?

43

A.J. IS OUR BOTANIST...
...HE'S INTERESTED IN ANYTHING THAT HAS TO DO WITH PLANTS.
ROSA IS CRAZY ABOUT MATH. SHE ALSO LIKES PHYSICS AND CHEMISTRY.
WEI LING IS A ZOOLOGY NUT-- SHE WANTS TO KNOW AS MUCH AS SHE CAN ABOUT ANIMALS.
I'M MOSTLY INTERESTED IN GEOLOGY-- THE STUDY OF ROCKS AND THE EARTH. BUT I LIKE ASTRONOMY, TOO.
WE LIKE TO DO EXPERIMENTS AND GO EXPLORING. TOGETHER, WE MAKE A PRETTY SMART GROUP.
HOW'S EVERYONE DOING? DO YOU WANT TO WORK A LITTLE MORE, OR SHOULD WE CALL IT A DAY?
I'M READY.
ME, TOO!
LET'S GO SCRUB SOME LIMESTONE.
YEP, IT'S A WHITE-CROWNED SPARROW.

Later in the afternoon . . .

And so, that night as the sun was setting...

48

Later that night . . .

By the second day, everyone had a pretty good idea what to do.

Later in the afternoon...

Later that evening, back at the cave . . .

During lunch the next day . . .

OKAY, WE'VE GOT A CAVE GHOST WE CAN USE ON TROGLOBRAINS, IF WE NEED TO. AND I THINK I COULD PAINT SOME PICTURES THAT SHOW HOW CAVES FORM. BUT WHAT IF WE WANT TO TEACH KIDS ABOUT STALACTITES, STALAGMITES AND OTHER SPELEOTHEMS?

KIDS? I BET THERE ARE PLENTY OF ADULTS WHO DON'T KNOW HOW SPELEOTHEMS FORM.

HOW ABOUT A SONG?

A SONG?

SURE! WHAT IF WE WRITE A ROCK AND ROLL SONG ABOUT SPELEOTHEMS?

OH RIGHT! AND WE COULD CALL OURSELVES THE STALACTITES...

NO, I THINK THIS WILL WORK. WHAT'S AN EASY-TO-REMEMBER TUNE?

CLEMENTINE!

OH, MY DARLING, OH, MY DARLING, OH, MY DARLING CLEMENTINE. YOU ARE LOST AND GONE FOREVER, DREADFUL SORRY, CLEMENTINE...

OKAY. NOW, WHAT IF WE CHANGE THE WORDS? HERE GOES:

IN A CAVERN, ON THE CEILING, WHERE THE BATS RETREAT AND HIDE...

62

So Grandpa finished explaining how stalactites and stalagmites are formed.

Later that afternoon...

IT'S LOOKING PRETTY GOOD IN HERE. ROSA, WHY DON'T YOU AND A.J. TAKE SOME OF THE BAGS OUT TO THE CAVE ENTRANCE. WE'LL KEEP SCRUBBING.

THEN WHEN YOU GET BACK, WE'LL HAUL THE REST OF THIS OUT TOGETHER.

IT'S GOOD TO SEE THAT TRASH WHERE IT BELONGS-- IN BAGS OUTSIDE THE CAVE.

NOW IF WE CAN JUST STOP TROGLOBRAINS FROM BRINGING ANY MORE GARBAGE IN...

EVEN THOUGH WE HAD FUN MAKING THE CAVE GHOST, IT'S NOT GOING TO STOP PEOPLE FROM VANDALIZING THE CAVE.

THAT'S RIGHT. THE GHOST MIGHT SCARE OFF THOSE TWO KIDS FOR AWHILE, BUT MAYBE THEY'LL DECIDE TO COME BACK WITH SOME OF THEIR FRIENDS.

THIS CAVE IS SO WELL KNOWN--AND IT'S ALREADY BEEN VISITED BY SO MANY PEOPLE WHO HAVEN'T TAKEN CARE OF IT.

I'M SURPRISED THERE ARE EVEN ANY BATS LEFT.

I HEARD LINDSEY'S GRANDPA SAY THAT SOMETIMES THE ONLY WAY TO PROTECT A CAVE LIKE THIS IS TO PUT A GATE ON IT. THAT WAY, THE CAVE OWNER WILL KNOW WHO'S GOING IN--AND CAN MAKE SURE THAT ONLY PEOPLE WHO CAVE SOFTLY ARE ALLOWED INSIDE.

BUT WHAT ABOUT THE BATS? IF THERE'S A GATE OVER THE ENTRANCE, HOW DO THEY GET IN OR OUT?

THE GATE IS BUILT WITH SPACES THAT ARE BIG ENOUGH FOR BATS TO FLY THROUGH.

HMMM, THAT SOUNDS LIKE JUST WHAT THIS CAVE NEEDS...

A.J. and Rosa explained what had happened.

72

Later in the evening . . .

80

84

Dear Matt and The Black Hole Gang,

Congratulations on discovering the new section of the cave. I can imagine how exciting that must have been. Keep up the good work on your clean-up and exploration.

I tried your recipe for speleothem pancakes, and they turned out well. Besides stalactites and stalagmites, I accidentally made a few columns.

Do you have any idea how much longer it will be until you're finished? I miss you—and all the neighborhood kids have been asking when you're coming home. Say "hi" to Lindsey and her Grandpa for me.

Love,
Dad

P.S. Give your mom a big hug from me.

Finally, it was time to say good-bye . . .

Two days and 900 miles later . . .